BLIND MOUNTAIN

Other books by Jane Resh Thomas

BLIND MOUNTAIN

by **Jane Resh Thomas**

CLARION BOOKS
New York

Clarion Books
a Houghton Mifflin Company imprint
215 Park Avenue South, New York, NY 10003
Copyright © 2006 by Jane Resh Thomas

The text was set in 13-point Eldorado

www.clarionbooks.com

Printed in the U.S.A.

Library of Congress Cataloging-in-Publication Data

Thomas, Jane Resh.
Blind mountain / by Jane Resh Thomas.
p. cm.
Summary: Unsure of himself and annoyed at having to spend a day
climbing a Montana mountain with his bossy father, twelve-year-old
Sam must become the guide on their perilous journey down
when his carelessness temporarily blinds his father.
ISBN-13: 978-0-618-64872-6
ISBN-10: 0-618-64872-0
[1. Fathers and sons—Fiction. 2. Self-confidence—Fiction.
3. Survival—Fiction. 4. Mountaineering—Fiction.
5. Montana—Fiction.] I. Title.
PZ7.T36695Bli 2006
[Fic]—dc22
2005034512

VB 10 9 8 7 6 5 4 3 2 1

To Pat Schmatz, who shares my love
of the word and the world,
with gratitude for her friendship

BLIND
MOUNTAIN

Chapter 1

SAM FLYNN TOSSED A FIST-SIZED rock and watched it tumble down the mountainside. It struck another rock, bounced wildly, and careened several feet in another direction. That's what would happen to Sam if he put his foot wrong, if he slipped, if a patch of brittle rock gave way beneath him.

"Hey!" His father called down from the sand-colored ledge where he stood. "Did you throw that rock, Sam?"

"No."

"Did you push it? Give it a little nudge? Set it in motion?"

Sam arranged a straight face to show his father and looked up the slope at him. "It's a rock," he said. "We're climbing. My boot must have loosened it."

"What if somebody was behind us, down below?"

Yeah. What if? What if Sam himself lost his balance? If he had followed the rock down the mountain, maybe his father would be sorry for making him come today. And who would hike behind them, anyway? Anybody with any brains would hike on a trail. But they were *Flynns*, weren't they? *Flynns* didn't take the easy road.

Their runty little border collie, Mac, hustled up beside Sam's father. The dog peered down and barked. His tongue hung out of his smiling mouth, and his feathery tail wagged his whole body. The boy and the dog had been partners since Sam was five and Mac a fuzzy black-and-white pup. *Come on!* he was saying now. *Hurry up. Isn't hiking fun?*

No. Hiking *wasn't* fun. Not anymore. Mac had been bred for keen intelligence and strenuous effort—for herding sheep from one field to another on the rugged moors of Scotland. The crumbly limestone cliffs here in the Montana Rockies were just another challenge to the dog. He and Sam's father had that in common. They both *liked* splashing across streams that plunged downhill in a froth. They *enjoyed* leaping from rocky ledge to stony shelf. The two of them could climb all day and not fall in a heap of fatigue at the end. Sam had been that way once, too, before he discovered the guitar. Before his father started razzing him all the time. Before he lost his nerve.

"Come on, damn it," called his father. "What's holding you up?"

"I'm coming as fast as I can," Sam yelled.

Ahead, still looking down at Sam from the ledge, his father leaned his cheek against the smooth blackthorn walking stick that Sam's mother had given him for his last birthday. These mountains reminded him of his boyhood in Scotland, he said, though they were higher and rougher than those back home, and he liked the easygoing people in the West. As soon as he had finished medical school and his surgery residency in New York, he had streaked out here.

Sam glanced up at Dad, who made a drama of waiting. As always, he was impatient. "I'm coming, I said," Sam repeated.

"Take your time, by all means."

The sarcastic edge in that voice made Sam's teeth hurt. As he hurried to catch up, his boot slipped in scree—the loose, eroded gravel that was always underfoot, rolling on the hard rock beneath it.

Sam's father met him at the edge of a cleft in the rock.

4

"We'll have to cross this little crack."

Sam approached the crevice, wary of slipping. It was wider than his arm was long, and too dark for him to see to the bottom.

"Little crack!" said Sam. "It's too wide."

"Barely thirty inches. Easy jump." Sam's father leapt across the crevice as easily as Mac. "See? Easy."

"What if I lose my footing?"

"Don't be a sissy. Come on."

"You go ahead. I'll wait here for you to come back," Sam said.

"Wait as long as you like, but I'll be going down a different way." Sam's father turned and strode away across a sloping patch of lavender asters.

Sam whimpered under his breath. What if he couldn't jump far enough to cross the split in the rock? He felt dizzy just imagining what would happen if he hadn't the strength, or he lost his nerve at the last minute, or his legs failed him. He would fall down to the dark bottom of the crack. His legs would break. The crevice was so deep, nobody would ever find him.

Looking back down the mountain at Sam, his father snorted, hands on his hips. "You've gone chicken since you joined that band."

Jab. Jab, jab—another of the constant swipes at Sam's music. Maybe Dad was— No, he couldn't be jealous of the band.

Dr. Flynn came back to the crevice. "Here. Take my hand."

Embarrassment burned in Sam. He wouldn't take his father's hand now if he were dangling off one of the hundred-foot cliffs on this mountain. "Go on!" he shouted. "I'll do it by myself."

His father turned his back again and went on alone. Sam looked down into the darkness. He kicked a stone. His wait for the clatter when it hit bottom was way too long.

Sam looked along the crack to see whether it narrowed. No—toward the river, the crevice broadened, and it continued in the other direction among some trees. Who knew how long it was? If Sam lost his way or took too much time looking for a narrow place, Dad would leave him behind.

Sam stepped back several feet, took a deep breath, ran toward the crevice, and jumped. He cleared it by at least a yard, and his momentum carried him on even after he landed. Falling forward and skidding on the rolling gravel, he scraped his knees and the palms of his hands. He shook the pain out of his hands and picked little stones out of shallow scratches. He was still alive. His jeans were torn and his knees oozed blood, but never mind—the bleeding would cleanse the wounds.

Still smiling, Mac found his way down Dad's trail to meet Sam. The dog licked his hand with one quick swipe, then ran behind him, clipping his knees, herding him, as if he were a slow sheep that had separated from the rest. Sam obeyed the dog and hurried to catch up with his father, who had gone out of sight. He hadn't even watched to make sure Sam was safe.

"Let's take a break here by the river," said Sam's father. He sat down and opened his pack, leaning against some kind of pine—Dad knew them all, but Sam never could remember the trees' names. His father squinted up at the sky. "We'll have to turn back soon."

Sam lay on his stomach and looked down at the rushing water. He felt like laughing. Too bad: they would have to go home. He couldn't wait.

His father prodded him with a sandwich. The smell of Cheddar cheese and mustard and bread and sweet pickles almost made Sam take the sandwich, but he wouldn't give in to hunger. He had jumped the crevice, and Dad hadn't even nodded. All he needed to say was "Good for you, Sam. Good job." Other fathers would have.

Sam hadn't wanted to hike in the first place, not when his friends were practicing for the middle-school concert in September. Robert Bailey was sitting in for Sam today. Maybe Robert played guitar better than Sam. Maybe the boys would keep Robert on and kick Sam out of the band.

A melancholy melody sang in Sam's mind. When the band had placed second in last year's music contest, Dad had said, "Only first counts," and turned away. Even a first wouldn't count, though. Dad hated rock music. In his eyes, artists of all kinds were girlish; if Sam wanted to play with his band, he must be a sissy, too. A mama's boy, Dad said.

He poked with the sandwich again. Sam's

hand moved against his will and accepted it, as if he were a robot and his stomach its master.

"Lighten up, can't you?" Dad sucked on a tube that led to a water bladder in his backpack. "These trips used to be fun."

Strange. Sam used to love the hikes, too—before Dad forced him to come along. But now that he was twelve and had a mind of his own, he wanted to hang out with his friends, not compete with Dad on these grueling climbs.

"If you live in the mountains, you need to know the mountains," his father went on. "Same as knowing the streets if you live in the city. When I was your age, I knew every corner in my Glasgow neighborhood, and every spring and boulder on Ben Lomond."

"Yeah, Dad, I'm sure. You were a hell of a guy."

"I told you, Sam, no backtalk. No swearing."

"You swear."

"Hey!" He poked Sam hard in the ribs with his boot. "I swear like a Scotsman, though."

Mac whined, waiting for his share of the sandwich. "Oh, all right," said Sam, handing over the last bite. Could Dad program a computer? Sam could. Could Dad deck Sam's judo teacher? Sam had done that once, too, even though it had been a lucky throw.

"Come on. You go first now," his father said. "No more rocks down the mountain. Do anything like that again, and you can find your own way home."

Sam dragged himself up the slope after Mac, grabbing aspen saplings or using firmly seated rocks as handholds. Mac looked back and herded Sam with the intensity of his gaze. His father herded him from behind. Everyone's eyes were on Sam, forward and back, as if he were livestock. Dad waited to pounce if he made a mistake. If only he could be in charge, just once, he would make Dad pay.

Sam walked up between some stunted pines that grew somehow out of the scrabble and rocks. He pushed between two small trees, breaking through the prickly branches with his arms up around his face. He grabbed a limb and walked on. Its sap smeared his hand. This sticky pine goo wouldn't wash off, no matter how hard he scrubbed, not until he cleaned his hand with turpentine back home. If he didn't remove every speck, his fingers would catch on the guitar strings. Disgusted, he let the pine bough go.

"Ahhh!"

Sam turned. His father was on his knees under one of the trees, clutching his face and swearing. "Bloody branch caught me right across the eyes," he groaned. "Never saw it coming."

Chapter 2

A MOMENT LATER, SAM'S FATHER began to yell. "Numbskull! Are you stupid, Sam? I've told you a million times . . ."

He rocked on his knees, his palms over his eyes.

"Dad, I'm sorry!"

"Can't see a bloody thing. Get your water pack." Sam's father shrugged off the straps of his backpack.

"It's empty."

"Then draw some water from my pack into my hands. Hurry up." Sam's father blinked and closed his eyelids and blinked again. Tears ran down the furrows of his face. He cupped his hands before him. Sam filled them with water, careful not to spill a drop.

As the water leaked between his fingers, Sam's father lowered his eyes into his cupped hands and then reared back. He groaned, his face a mask of pain. He lifted his head and opened his eyes but quickly shut them again, wincing. "Can't stand the glare."

"More water?"

"Doubt it would help."

"Try. Open your eyes again in the water."

"All right, I'll try." Sam's father washed his eyes again, blinked again, and shut them again against the glare. "You have to help me, Sam."

"Anything. Tell me what to do."

"Find a stick the size of a pencil."

Sam picked up a small stick. "Got it."

"Make sure it's clean. All I need is more ragtag in my eyes."

Sam rubbed the stick on his jeans until it was worn smooth and no more bark fell off.

Sam's father talked now in his surgeon mode, the way he spoke to his patients on the phone, formal and certain. "Lay the stick across the lid, catch the lashes between your finger and thumb, and flip the lid back over the stick."

As if Sam hadn't flipped his own eyelid a million times. He tried to do as his father said, but his yelling earlier had made Sam nervous and clumsy.

"Not like that!" his father snapped.

Sam flinched.

"Follow directions, for once in your life."

"I'm doing the best I can." Sam swallowed his irritation and tried to open his father's left eyelid, but the strong muscles clenched it shut.

"Try again," said Sam's father in a quieter voice. "I'll relax."

This time the maneuver worked. Sam's stomach flipped. The red meat of his own eye socket was one thing, but Dad's was another.

"Is the eyeball clean?"

"Nothing on it. Yes, clean."

"I'll hold my eyelid open with my fingers. You squirt it with water."

Sam let water flow through the tube from the reservoir in his father's pack.

Sam's father felt for the tube, squirted some water into his open eye, and flipped his lid back into place.

"Other eye."

Sam did the same with the right eye.

His father sat up, blinking and mouthing all the curses he didn't want Sam to say. Open and shut. Open and shut. He struck his thigh with his hand. His eyes were swollen now and very red. Tears streamed down his face.

"What is it?" said Sam. "Are you crying?"

"Damn it, Sam! My eyes are watering. You've blinded me," Sam's father shouted. "Cursed pine needles scratched the corneas."

Sam tried to shut out the image in his mind—Dad, picking his way across a busy street with a white cane. For the rest of both their lives, Dad's blindness would be Sam's fault. "Will your eyes heal?" he whispered.

"They'll heal. Antibiotics are a wonderful thing. But Sam, you'll have to get us down."

"Down?"

"Down off this mountain."

"Me?" said Sam. "I have to get us down?"

"Yup. You have to get us down."

Sam cringed. "We can go hungry for a while and get water from the stream. I'll build us a lean-to. We'll wait for your eyes to heal."

"This was just a day trip, Sam. Away by dawn, home by six. You know we didn't bring supplies for camping. You didn't even bring water."

They had climbed steadily all morning. Now they were miles from the road where they had left the car, and hundreds of feet higher up the mountain. The way up had been the hard way, bushwhacking where no trail existed, up rocks and across streams. Dad *always* did everything the hard way. How would Sam find the way down?

"My eyes'll soon be infected, anyway," Dad said. "We have to go down now."

"But what if I can't?"

"You have to. No choice. We've climbed since you were three. We'll find out now whether you paid attention."

"But Dad—"

"Go back exactly the way we came."

Of course. Do just exactly as Dad did. As if Sam had actually noticed the way they came. He imagined himself stepping on a small stone. It rolled under his feet. He lost his balance and began to slide, pulling his father off his feet as well. They slid together in a cloud of dust to the edge of a cliff and—

Mac licked Sam's hand, bringing him out of his daydream. Smarter about the mountains than any human, the dog had never failed Sam yet. Mac would help him. Mac would lead, and Sam would follow. The two of them would find the way home. Then Dad would *have* to admire him.

Sam looked around the slope. It was gentle here. All he would have to do is head downhill.

He stood up and stretched on tiptoe to settle his father's backpack on his broad shoulders. Sam put his arms through the harness of his own pack, shifted it until it set comfortably on his shoulders, and handed his father his blackthorn stick.

"All right, then," said Sam. "Let's go."

Chapter 3

WHEN THEY EMERGED FROM THE stand of pines, Sam surveyed the downward slope. Nothing hinted that any human being had ever passed this way. Scrubby gray-green plants and sharp tan grasses had sprung erect again, unbroken by their feet on the way up. Off to their right, the river's bluster was the only sign of where they were. No paved highways for the *Flynns*.

"See, Dad," Sam said. "You should have listened to me this morning. The trails have maps. Why do we always have to bushwhack?"

"You're right, Sam. A trail would be a blessing, but you know how I hate to hike in Times Square."

"What?"

"Times Square. Traffic jams. New York, where I learned surgery—must have been crazy to go there. Mom and I came to Montana just after you were born."

As if Sam didn't know the family history by heart. He resumed his complaint. "On a trail, we could have met somebody to help us."

"You're entirely right, my boy. But now we have to find our way down on our own."

"We could yell for help. We could whistle."

"Who would hear us?" said Sam's father. "I come up here to get away from people and cell phones. Come on, then—we might as well get cracking."

Now he sounded as reasonable as anybody could, even cheerful. He liked nothing better than a challenge. But Sam was far from cheerful. Oh, why had he let that branch fly? He considered the lay of the land. They would take a zigzag diagonal route to reduce the angle of their descent down the slope, moving one way, and then the other.

"Put your foot down to the right, Dad. You'll feel a tree branch."

Sam's father grasped the branch and held it while he inched down the slope. In some places the rock was exposed, with little vegetation. Elsewhere, in bowls where eroded soil had collected, where rain and river mist could sprout the seeds and water the plants, gaillardias flaunted flowers that resembled red-and-yellow daisies. Lupines, like blue sweet peas, moved in the wind. Sam surprised himself, seeing details he had missed before. He could identify more plants and trees than he had realized.

"Over here now, sideways, Dad. Sit down

and hang on to the rock. The drop is only a couple feet."

Dad felt his way onto the rock with his hands, then turned over on his stomach and felt with his foot for solid ground below. He obeyed every instruction exactly. For once in his life, *Sam* was boss, telling *Dad* every move to make. . . . Sam could leave *him* here to find his own way home. But of course Dad had just been talking when he had threatened to leave Sam at the crevice. Dad would never abandon Sam, and Sam would never leave his father.

"Here, Dad. We're going crosswise down a big bald outcropping. Nothing here to hang on to—just patches of moss and lichen. But the slope isn't very steep."

They inched along. Beyond the bald rock, they made their way over scree. Sam watched ahead for the easiest way down. His father clutched the blackthorn with one hand and extended the other to keep his balance, feeling for every step with his feet. Mac had slowed to match the pace Sam set. He bustled on ahead, then returned to run behind Sam and his father, rounding them up. Then, ears perked, Mac waited between the trees for Sam to follow.

After a while, they stopped to rest in the shade of enormous Douglas firs, just standing still, catching their breath.

"You're trembling," said Sam.

"I'm all right. My muscles are tense from the effort of keeping upright."

"Dad, we don't have much water left. We'll have to go down to the river." The stream was the same one that had come in and out of view all morning. "I catch a glitter of water now. Getting down looks easy," said Sam.

"Would that it were. . . . Okay. Let's go."

"We're coming through the trees into a little clearing, Dad. The ground is fairly level here.

Take my hand. I'll hold the branches for you," said Sam. "I'll be careful." How could he have let a branch slap his father in the face?

The slope fell gradually through the clearing, but at the other side were craggy rocks.

"Careful. Here's the crevice we jumped earlier," said Sam. Returning to this place had taken three or four times longer than the upward trek.

Sam's fear was a soccer ball in his throat. Maybe they could take another route. He looked up at the sky to estimate the time of day. Too late. The sun had slid down behind the mountain too far. It must be about three o'clock, and Sam and his father were descending the eastern slope of the mountain, where shadows deepened early and suddenly. Sam didn't have time to look for a place where the split might peter out and the two faces of rock join up.

They would have to jump the chasm again.

"Stand still a minute." Sam put his hands on his father's shoulders and turned him to face the crevice square. "You'll have to jump straight ahead. Wait now. I'll go first." Sam gauged the thirty-inch split once more. His hands still stung from the last jump, and the blood from his scraped knees had dried stiff on his jeans.

Sam took two steps back and tensed to control his trembling. He trembled anyway. He gathered his courage, ran, and leapt. This time he didn't fall, and again he landed at least a yard beyond the other lip of the split. He was a better jumper than he thought. "I'm across!" he shouted.

"Well, well. So you found a little heart."

Jab.

Now Sam's father prepared himself. He hesitated. He tested the ground with his stick, found the air between the rocks, and gauged it. "Good thing I'm a daddy longlegs," he said, but he didn't jump. His hands trembled just like Sam's.

Sam couldn't resist. "Don't be a sissy," he said. "You can do it."

His father took a breath, ready to leap, but he stopped at the last moment. "Yikes!" he said.

"Don't be a baby, Dad." Sam began to like this role. "Find a little heart."

"Lay off, will you? I get the point."

"*You* don't lay off. You never lay off!" said Sam.

Sweat dripped from his father's eyebrows and the tip of his nose.

"Come on, baby," said Sam. "Jump the cliff. You can do it."

His jaws bulging with the strain of set teeth, Sam's father used the blackthorn to feel the distance between his feet and the near edge of the crevice.

"Six inches," Sam said.

Dad felt the air between the edges of rock again.

"Thirty inches," said Sam. A twinge of pity stirred in him. "Take my hand." He reached across the divide and took his father's wrist.

His father wrenched his hand away and tensed again, ready to jump. At the last moment, he stopped himself and fell to his knees.

Shame washed over Sam. "Please, Dad. Take my hand."

His father stood and tried to open his eyes. "Can't see a bleedin' thing," he said.

Sam couldn't tell whether his father was weeping or his eyes were watering from the injury.

He reached out and felt for Sam.

Making sure his sneakers wouldn't slip on loose gravel, Sam set his feet and leaned across to take his father's hand in his own.

His father stood poised for a moment. "Now!" he said. He leapt. Sam pulled. They were both safely across the divide.

Chapter 4

Sitting down heavily, Sam's father groaned. His whole body shook. "Legs won't hold me up. I hope we don't meet many more of those."

"Yeah," Sam said, nodding his head at the thought. They would certainly encounter even worse hazards, unless he could find exactly the same way down that they had taken up the mountain. But that path was lost now to the wind and shifting grasses.

"What time is it?" His father held out his wrist so Sam could see his watch.

"Nearly four." Nearly four. They had hardly

begun their descent. They would have to camp.

"We'll have to camp," Sam's father said.

There he went again, telling Sam something he already knew perfectly well. Did Dad think he was an idiot?

"How much food do you have left?" asked Dad.

"Enough," Sam lied.

"When I reminded you to put in your share this morning, you didn't do it, did you?"

Sam shifted his shoulders under his light pack.

"Well?"

"Get off my back, Dad." Sam was guilty as charged. Sometimes he tried to follow Dad's directions, but he couldn't help pulling the other way. Sometimes he simply forgot things. Sometimes disobedience just felt good. If he was lucky, maybe he had some jerky left over from the last hike in the mountains, maybe a couple of ounces. There might be some nuts. A few dried apricots. He couldn't look now. Dad would hear the zipper open and ask for details.

Nearby a woodpecker hammered a tree and then flew overhead in a peculiar, dipping flight. Behind the bird's *ratatat,* Sam heard a roaring.

"Listen," he said.

Off to the right, water rushed over rock, now in a fiercer mood, changing with the slope of the mountain. They would make camp beside the river overnight. They would replenish their water, and in the morning, rested, they would continue on home. Maybe by morning, Dad would even be able to see.

"We can camp by the river," Sam's father said. "At least we'll have water."

"Duh!" said Sam under his breath. "This

way." He yanked on his father's flannel shirt sleeve.

"What'd you say?"

"I said, 'Yeah.'"

Sam's father grabbed his wrist and twisted it. "No backtalk. I'm still in charge here."

That's where Dad was wrong. Sam rubbed his wrist. He really *could* walk away, he could walk away whenever he wanted. Let Dad be afraid for a change and see how he liked it. Let the forest rangers— Sam stopped himself in the middle of the thought. Nursing his resentment wouldn't get them home.

Gathering himself again, Sam looked for a place to camp. He led the way to the right, stopping every few steps to listen for water. As they walked, the sound grew louder. The ground sloped more sharply. Maybe he could find a path to the river that wasn't too steep. He zigzagged his way down, grabbing cedar trees for holds with one hand, as his father followed on his belly, feet first. Sam steadied him with his other hand pressed flat on his father's backside. Before long, the slope eased, and his father could stand up.

The trees here grew close together and engulfed them in a cloud of scent that smelled spicy, just like Mom's cedar chest, where she kept their wool clothes in the summer. The bark of the trees was shaggy gray, with just a hint of the wood's interior rosiness. Sam hadn't come hiking with Dad for several weeks. He had missed this powerful smell.

Sam stopped a moment to watch how his father used his blackthorn. Still face down, he maneuvered the stick crosswise between trees for support. Some wood hardens as it ages, his father had said; old blackthorn was nearly as hard as iron, and it wasn't brittle. Now it served as an overhead bar, distributing his weight between two or several trees, more secure than if he depended on just one. He tested the ground ahead with the stick, driving its tip into soft soil or between rocks, as if it were a third leg. Dad knew how to use a stick—Sam had to grant him that.

Sam paused and shut his eyes. How would it feel to be blind on this steep incline? He tested for solid footing, hanging on to a sapling with one hand. He stroked the air, feeling for something, anything, to support his weight. Blindness was too terrifying—he had to give up and open his eyes after only a few seconds. He'd have to give Dad credit for a lot more than handling a stick. Climbing down a bluff, blind, would be the scariest thing in the world.

As they picked their way down the steep slope, Sam could see the river glistening between trees. After the water turned a corner, it flowed flat for a considerable distance before it fell off into space, throwing up a cloud of mist. Sam had seen this waterfall before, from below, its drop so deep and sudden, it made him queasy to look at it. Here above, the stream flowed more slowly on the near bank, the inner curve of a bend, a pool still enough for sedge and horsetails to grow in the sandy verge. Some of the rocks here were flat. The spot would make a good place for them to camp. Sam would fill the water packs, and maybe even swim.

He helped his father inch down the last several yards. "We're down, Dad. Sit here." He shoved together a pile of pine needles.

His father cupped his hand around his ear. "Can't hear over the noise of the falls," he yelled.

Sam spoke, close to his father's head. "We're down. Sit here awhile. I want to look around." He eased his father down onto the pine needles.

"Don't drink from the river, Sam," his father warned. "Don't forget giardia. All we need now is a nice case of diarrhea."

"Yeah, Dad!" Sam shouted.

When his father was settled, Sam carried their backpacks across the small rocks to the water's edge forty or so yards from the bottom of the slope. He looked around. The river, wild and deep with melted snow, must scour this bank every spring, uprooting any baby trees that tried to grow. Sam drank directly from the stream, ignoring the pain in his hands and knees, plunging his face full into the water. Nothing had ever tasted so good as the cold water from this mountain stream. He would take his chances on giardia. If Dad wanted to drink lukewarm water from the pack, good for him.

But Sam had second thoughts. Risking parasites for the sake of defiance was dumb. He wiped his lips and spat out every drop he could suck from his mouth. He poured the old water out of the storage bladders inside the backpacks and took out his father's hand pump. With one of its tubes in the river and the other in the backpack's reservoir, he pumped water through the filter until both bladders were full. Good. Now they each had three liters of clean water that wouldn't make them sick.

Later, he would strip off his clothes and wash off his sweat in the pool. To check it for safety, he tossed a little stick into the water there. It floated lazily for a few feet until an eddy caught it, toyed with it for a few whirlpool turns, then flung it into the main current, which swept it away to the waterfall in an instant. This pool was not for swimming.

Sam poked in the sedge that grew at the boggy edges of the river a few feet upstream. The farther he went along the riverbank, the easier the grade was up the slope from the river; he had picked the hardest spot to descend. Before long, he came to a rivulet of spring water flowing through dark sand into the river. There, sunk deep into the sand, was an animal track, much too big for a deer, and not a hoof-print, anyway. It was big, but not big enough or long enough to be a grizzly's track. Something heavy, though.

Where was Mac? He would sense danger before Sam saw or heard a thing. Sam's heartbeat clogged his throat as he looked up the slope and behind him along the river's edge. He scanned his memory for the pages of tracks in his *Boy Scout Handbook* and the *U.S. Army Survival Manual* his father had given him for Christmas last year—another attempt to make a mighty hunter of him, rather than a musician. Sam remembered clearly the animal tracks printed in the books, but this one was too indistinct to identify. Maybe the animal had been a deer after all, and the water had eroded the depression in the sand, enlarging it. Maybe Sam was just a scaredy-cat, as Dad always told him.

Watching his back, Sam explored upstream a few feet farther, where the sedge grew more sparsely and the wet sand was shallow over the underlying rock. There . . . another track. This was certainly no bear track; it was too perfectly round. Sam knelt for a closer look. The cool, damp sand soothed his injured knees, bruised and scabby though they were. He was sure the imprint was not a coyote or a wolf track, either. In winter, if they were hungry, coyotes nosed around for scraps behind the grocery store, where the butcher sometimes forgot to clamp the lid down tight on the Dumpster. And Sam had seen the tracks of wolves so many times, he could distinguish them from dog and coyote tracks. No, this one was broader and rounder than a wolf track. It was feline, he was sure. And big—definitely big.

It could be a lynx track. Or the track of a mountain lion—a cougar.

The cougar was as dangerous as any animal in these mountains—maybe, in its stealth and speed, even more dangerous than a grizzly. Sam jumped to his feet and looked over his shoulder as Mac came up behind him to herd him back to his father. A low growl rattled in the dog's throat. He shouldered Sam with urgent insistence. Running now, Sam picked up the backpacks from the river's edge and returned to the site he had picked for a camp. He wanted the illusory safety of numbers. Every time he bent his knees, the wounds from his first jump across the cleft hurt and oozed a little more. A cougar would smell the blood. Sam's father was bloody, too, and defenseless.

Back at the camp, Dad lay on the pine needles, his back against the slope, one arm across his face over the bandanna he had knotted to cover his eyes. Some safety. Dad couldn't protect him from an ant. Any protection would have to come from Sam himself. From Sam, who Dad said was afraid of his own shadow. Sam the sissy.

"Sam?"

He didn't want to scare Dad. Besides, if he was wrong about the track, Dad would never let him forget his mistake. Pretending he hadn't seen anything would be easy, if he could just catch his breath. "I'm back, Dad." He spoke into his father's face. "This place is open rock with a clear view in all directions."

"You scouted. Good. What did you find, Sam?"

"Nothing much."

"We need water, but you have to make camp, and I'm too tired. We have enough until morning." Dad leaned back against a rock. "Remember, don't drink from the river."

"Quit worrying so much about a little parasite," said Sam. "I drink from the river all the time. If giardia was in the river, I'd have it by now." Then he relented. "I already filled the packs with the pump."

Dad would not give up the bickering. "If you hadn't let that branch go, I wouldn't have to worry. We'd be home, drinking water from the tap."

"If you hadn't followed so close, the branch wouldn't have hit you." Throwing the mean words back in Dad's face made Sam swell with his own power, but he didn't have time to gloat.

Sam looked at the watch on his father's wrist. Nearly five. He would have to hurry. He put his fingers together between his lips and whistled the shrill call his father had taught him. Mac thrashed through the brush a few yards upstream, crossed the broken rock, and lay down beside Sam's father. Mac never lay down voluntarily if he could find anything else to do. The climbing today had hardly winded him, but now he was sticking close by, like a guard. He must know things Sam didn't know about the cougar.

"Keep him here with you, Dad." Sam patted the dog's black head, took his white muzzle in his hand, and looked him in the eyes. "Stay, Mac. Stay with Dad."

"What did you see over there? You sound worried."

"Nothing, Dad. Just keep Mac with you, in case."

"In case of what? Don't be such a worry-wart."

"Okay, Dad. But what if a bear or something *did* nose around here? Would you build the fire away from the brush or away from the noise of the falls?" Sam asked. "We'd never hear a predator in this spot."

"What if?" said his father. "I'm more afraid of a forest fire than I am of any animal. And Mac would smell a predator, even if he couldn't hear it. What did you see when you scouted, Sam?"

"I guess I am a worrywart. You always say so. Give me your hatchet, Dad. I'm going to cut some boughs and gather firewood while it's still light."

His father handed over the hatchet. "Think about every step and every chop before you make it," he said. "We can't afford another injury."

"Yeah, Dad. Tell me about it. And Dad— take your knife out of its sheath. Keep it by you."

"Why?"

Sam ignored the question. Responsibility weighed heavy in his stomach as he headed into the trees again. He would have to ignore his father's bossing, too. It was habit—both the bossing and Sam's own opposition. All Dad's hopes and all Mom's mothering had gone into Sam, the only child, cramping him so tight he couldn't move. He was in charge now, though. He was boss—just what he had always wanted. Or thought he wanted.

Shivering, Sam glanced behind him. Think about every step. We can't afford another injury. Dad had no idea of the danger that waited for them, somewhere in those woods.

Chapter 5

AS SAM CLAMBERED AMONG THE trees above his father, he was very careful. A cut shin would be a disaster for them all—his father, Mac, and Sam himself. He stood still and tested the hatchet's edge with his thumb. It was almost as sharp as the Swiss Army knife he wore tied with a shoelace to a belt loop at his waist. Dad never did anything halfway.

Stopping every other minute to look down at his father and scan the woods around him, he cut green cedar boughs and hauled them back to the campsite for a bed, thinking before every step and every chop. His hands and arms, sticky all over with sap, clung to everything. Oh, *why* had he been so squeamish about that little smear of pine sap earlier; *why* had he let go of that branch? He kicked a pebble, but the waterfall's incessant noise drowned out the sound of the clattering stone.

He trimmed the boughs and piled up the greens near a shallow depression in the limestone that could serve as a fire pit, slightly protected from the wind by loose rocks. A sedimentary rock, the limestone had accumulated in thin layers millions of years ago, when water submerged this whole region. Minerals settled out of the water on the bottom, gradually building, and then movements of the earth heaved the mountains up. Fossil hunters found sea creatures' remains even on mountain tops.

The scaly stone flaked fairly easily as Sam deepened the pit with the back of the hatchet head. The campsite was far enough away that no stray spark from the fire could ignite dry brush.

Dad still sat at the foot of the slope as Sam built a springy bed of cedar boughs. Shoving the hatchet handle into the waistband of his jeans, he went back to the trees for firewood. Nothing grew here at the riverside but cedar and aspen and a few firs, and that wood burned quickly. Half surprised that he knew a few things without his father's prompting, Sam considered that an all-night fire would eat a lot of logs. He looked for dead aspen saplings that had sprouted among the cedars and died for want of sun and nutrients. He wanted little trees or blowdowns that had hung up in branches when they fell. These would be dry and would not have rotted yet. Stumbling in his haste, he hauled several of them to the fire pit.

Even though he broke off as many branches as he could, none of the logs was very manageable, and Sam didn't have time to chop them into shorter pieces before night fell. He would have to feed the dead trees into the fire as they burned away. He went back into the trees again and again for more wood, avoiding over-hanging rocks and thick brush. He was shaking now.

By the time he had gathered twice as many logs as he thought they would need, deep shadow had engulfed the woods, and even the open campsite was dusky. The air was already cold. Sam saw himself, armed only with his knife and his father's hatchet, fending off a cougar, its mouth agape and its teeth shiny ivory daggers. Glancing over his shoulder, he hauled in one more aspen sapling, just to be certain, and hurried back to his father. Even he would give high marks to the camp Sam had made.

"I've collected the firewood," Sam said in his father's ear.

"Gather twice as much as you think you need, Sam. Nights in the mountains are cold."

Sam stepped back. "Right, Dad. Thanks for explaining." He could be as smart mouthed as he wanted; Dad couldn't hear a word over the waterfall's noise unless Sam was in his face. He didn't think Sam could spell his own name, but here he was, protecting both of them, and Mac besides. Sam shuddered. Now that he had the power, what if he failed? If his father was right about him, they were all in a fine fix. Maybe he should ask for advice about the cat.

"Come on," Sam said, close enough to his father's neck to smell his body's distinctive scent and traces of his aftershave. "Let's move to the campsite." He picked up the little pile of fine kindling his father had gathered and pulled him to his feet. Dad put his hand on Sam's shoulder. They both walked unsteadily in the dim light, tripping on loose rocks and slipping on scree. Sam stepped into a slight dip that he hadn't noticed. The sudden drop jolted his whole body. Being blind like Dad, even crossing fairly flat rocks would be terrifying.

Sam led his father to a rock near the cedar-bough bed. "You can sit down here."

Dad sat down on the scaly rock. He inspected the boughs by touch.

"This bed is pretty good. Now build a fire that's just as careful."

"Dad, I get nervous when people tell me every move to make," said Sam, leaning in. "Trust me. I can build a fire."

"I know the guy who taught you woodcraft, so I guess I do. I do trust you."

There he went, taking credit for everything Sam knew. Sam stuffed his anger and criss-crossed his father's kindling above dead pine needles in the shallow depression. He laid slightly larger broken branches on top. One match lit the pine sap oozing from the end of a twig, which he placed among the needles at the bottom. Other small gooey sticks caught fire from the needles, then larger wood glowed and burst into flame. Soon the fire blazed. Sam watched the sparks rise against the darkening sky. The fire was a good one that wouldn't gutter out, and the sparks died long before they could start a forest fire. He smiled.

"Watch out that the sparks don't set fire to brush in the woods," Dad said.

"Great, Dad, thanks!" Sam said under his breath. "I never thought of that." The strain was getting to Sam.

While he waited for a bed of coals to form, he considered the excellence of the fire he had built. He, too, knew the guy who had taught him woodcraft. A long time ago, when Sam was a little kid, he had loved nothing better than bushwhacking and camping with his father. Before he was ten, Sam could keep up with Dad and other men on backpacking trips up this mountain and even more rugged ones.

Then Sam began to have his own ideas. He killed his first buck, but he threw up and couldn't gut him. He might hunt again someday, but not now. Silly, Dad said. Then Sam began taking guitar lessons from the music teacher at school. Sam was a natural, the teacher said. Soon Sam wanted to play dark music with his band when his father wanted to hike. The more Sam resisted, the more Dad pushed. He began to ridicule Sam—only mamas' boys wanted to lie around the house, he said. The meaner Dad was, the more Mom defended Sam, and the more they all argued, the more he doubted himself. Gradually, the distance between Sam and his father had widened until it was like the cleft in the rock.

Now by the fire, Sam opened his father's

backpack again. It was full of gear in addition to the water pack. He found a waterproof nylon ground sheet. He laid it over the green boughs and anchored all four corners with loose rocks. Folded in the bottom of the pack was a pair of big space blankets, the thin covers that took up hardly any room, but would trap most of a person's body heat. These silvery blankets wouldn't keep them very warm, but at least they wouldn't freeze.

Nice going, Dad. One more worry evaporated from Sam's mind.

The fire would keep big predators away. Sam relaxed as he sorted through the gear. Among the other equipment was a compass, Dad's big flashlight, and a beeswax candle; beeswax burned longer than paraffin. Dad had also packed a bag of trail mix with a lot of raisins and nuts, two giant Hershey bars, and a brick of Cheddar cheese—sharp Cheddar.

Dad couldn't live without his cheese; sometimes he sent away for the stinky kind.

At the pack's bottom was a large package of jerky Mom had made. Mom. She would expect them home now. She would alert the rangers. Tomorrow morning rescuers would find them—If the cougar didn't get them first. Sam tried to remember whether cougars prowled by day or night. Night, probably, and the whole long night lay ahead of them.

Mac sniffed the air and paced at the edge of the firelight. He was worried, too.

Sam shoved the big end of a tree in among the coals. It caught fire quickly. All the dead saplings were dry and quick to flame up.

From the bottom of his own pack, Sam salvaged a small piece of jerky, one brittle dried apricot, and seven jellybeans, everything shaggy with lint. For an instant, Sam was glad his father couldn't see to compare Sam's provisions with his own. He was already wearing his fleece parka. Shivering, Sam pulled his own fleece over his head.

"Your eyes?" Sam asked. His father just shook his head. Tired of shouting to be heard, now they hardly talked.

Sam put good food and the drinking tube under his father's hands. He ate the fuzzy apricot and the antique jerky and candy himself, a penance for his carelessness. His father ate a bit of cheese, a handful of trail mix, and one bite of the newly dried meat, drank his fill, and lay down on the bed. Dad was conserving food. He wasn't sure they would reach home soon. Sam shuddered.

He soaked several bites of jerky for Mac in a shallow dip in the rock. The dog ate the meat and a piece of cheese in a couple of bites, and then paced again at the camp's edge, staring out into the night, his ears perked forward, occasionally growling.

"Where's that dog?" Sam's father asked. "I

don't like the way he's acting. He's spooked."

"He's right here." Sam changed the subject. "What do you think Mom's doing now?"

"Oh, she's probably damping down the fire in Barb's stove, getting ready for bed. She and Barb were going with a couple of friends to the cabin for the weekend."

"Aunt Barb's cabin? They don't even have a phone there. Did Mom take the cell phone?"

"Probably not. They like roughing it."

"Oh, that's just great. Now nobody will know we didn't get home tonight."

"Right, boyo. We're on our own."

Sam stared into the woods, looking for eyes, the glitter of eyes. Dad would know what to do about a cougar. If he knew about the track, he would be ready to defend them.

"Dad. What would you do if you thought a big cat was out there?"

His father opened his eyes and squinted at

Sam, but they watered so much in the fire's glare and smoke, he closed them again and lay back on the pine boughs. "Look, Sam, are you worried about nothing? Or did you see something when you scouted?"

"Maybe something. Maybe a track."

"How big a track?"

"Four inches. Maybe more. Way bigger than my palm."

"You're sure it was a cat?"

"Pretty sure."

"Bigger than your hand? It's a cougar, then," said Dad. "Why didn't you tell me, Sam? How far is the nearest overhang?"

"Back in the trees. Maybe fifty feet from camp."

"You've already done everything we can do," Dad said. "You built a fire—even over the waterfall noise, I can hear that it's good. You laid the bed close, and no cougar will brave a fire." He felt for his knife on his belt. "Keep your knife and the hatchet ready. Keep Mac in camp."

As Sam felt at his waist, his stomach sank to his knees. No hatchet. No weapon at all except his jackknife. The Swiss Army knife's corkscrews and screwdrivers were useless.

"You know cats are always a threat up here," said Dad. "You're just more alert now."

Where had Sam used the hatchet last? Chopping off boughs? No, after that, right here in camp, he had trimmed loose bark off the dead saplings for kindling. The cougar could be out there now, watching him, waiting to pounce as soon as he turned his back. It might have crept to the other side of the woodpile while he was looking somewhere else. When he bent to look under the brush, the cougar would rush him. A kid, even with a knife, wouldn't have a prayer.

He stood at the edge of firelight, directing the beam of the flashlight around the pile of dead trees four or five feet from the fire. No hatchet lay there, and the moment the beam moved, the cougar might slink into the shadows where Sam had just checked. His eyes smarted from the smoke of the fire. He squatted to look under the brush, but he couldn't see far into the snarl of logs and branches, and the hatchet might be on the other side. What a screwup he was.

Sam called Mac to his side with a hand gesture. Mac would help him. Mac would smell the cat, even if Sam couldn't see it. They crept around the perimeter of the firewood together, Sam watching over his shoulder, then casting the light on the dark side of the brush. Mac stayed glued to Sam's knee, alert, ears pricked, but not growling. Mac would bark if the cougar was near. Still, Sam thought he was going to throw up. Although he hadn't found the hatchet, he returned with Mac to the safety of the fire. He was in charge now—and he had botched the job.

His father lay with his forearm resting on his eyes, snoring softly. Cat or no cat, the strain of walking blind had caught up with him. Sam covered him with one of the space sheets and tucked him in. The strangest impulse came over Sam then, to kiss Dad on his forehead, as he himself used to kiss Sam at bedtime. His father stirred slightly but didn't wake up.

Mac lay down at the edge of the bed, his eyelids half closed. Surely the dog sensed no danger.

With the flashlight in one hand and the jackknife in the other, Sam walked a few feet away from the fire to look up at a million stars. Now, in August, the Perseid meteor shower was at its height; shooting stars jetted across the sky every night. There went one now, inviting a wish. Sam whispered his heart's desire—not a new computer game this time; not wild applause for the band at the concert; not a kiss from Sarah Jameson the next time the gang went to a movie. Just let Dad's eyes heal. Let them all reach home safely.

The stars and the scent of burning pine awoke memories of other campsites, of Dad's friends laughing at a joke, of sharing the work, of enjoying the company of men. Their sons, they said, had found new interests, buddies, girls. Older boys stayed home, no longer willing to miss whole weekends of soccer matches and hockey and dances and competitive computer games. Two years ago, his father's friends had looked at him with some kind of longing. One of them had ruffled Sam's hair once and wondered aloud what his own son was doing at that moment. Even then Sam had longed to be home with the guys, his own friends.

Mac appeared at Sam's side, his ears pricked and the soft hair on his ruff and back raised. The dog stared intently upstream, toward the spring and the woods.

The hair on Sam's neck rose, too. "What's the matter, boy?" Sam put his face beside Mac's head. A low growl rumbled in the dog's throat, a vibration Sam could feel on his cheek. The dog ran out a few feet from Sam, barking, his nose high, smelling the wind. He stopped, one forefoot bent in the air, as if prepared to sprint, all his senses focused in a pinpoint of attention. Then he came back to Sam, shouldering him again. Sam needed no urging.

From the edge of the camp he shone the flashlight between the trees, inching the beam along the ground. Still nothing. Mac growled again and watched. Sam aimed the flashlight straight ahead along the line of his dog's gaze. Nothing. But Mac was never wrong. Maybe a cougar would climb. Sam aimed the beam higher, lighting up rocky shelves, then higher yet, up into the trees.

Something waited out there in the dark, Sam was sure, something he couldn't see.

Chapter 6

SAM PLACED THE BOTTOM ENDS of two more snapped-off trees in the fire. Twigs flared up. He had been watching for hours, sitting on sticky boughs and leaning back against the pine bed, the second blanket wrapped around Mac and himself. Occasionally he got up to move the burning saplings into the fire pit. He had removed his knife from its shoestring and held it, open now, in his hand. Putting his arm around Mac's neck, Sam pulled the blanket up around their heads, fighting fatigue. The strain had worn him out, too. Even after an ordinary day in the mountains, he always fell asleep as soon as he sat down.

The next thing he knew, he awoke with a jerk that pulled a painful muscle in his neck and shook his whole body. He rubbed his neck with both hands. What had awakened him? Some sound? Where he had breathed on a wrinkle of the silvery sheet, ice crystals had made a pretty pattern.

Sam shone the flashlight around the campsite and swept the beam across the nearest trees. An early blast of the coming winter had blown in while he slept. Clouds covered the stars entirely now. The mist from the waterfall had frozen in a fuzzy rime on every surface. Every branch and needle of the pines near the falls was three times fatter than normal. The woods and the stretch of scattered rocks were fairyland.

Great. Now they would have to walk on ice.

Mac had already shrugged off the blanket to patrol the campsite's perimeter. Sam stretched his muscles, flexed his stiff joints, and stood up. He yawned, but Mac was entirely awake. He rushed away from the fire, barking loudly. Before Sam could pick him out with the beam of the flashlight, Mac ran back to nudge Sam nearer his father.

"Sit." Mac sat. "Stay."

Dad sat up abruptly. "What's all the foo-faraw?"

"Dunno."

Sam shoved the ends of the logs farther into the fire, relieved that the embers were deep and still alive. The fire had not gone out while he slept. He couldn't have slept for long, then.

Mac growled and barked again, an alarm bark, frantic and wild, but he stayed by Sam's father, who stood now by the pine-bough bed. Sam shone the flashlight into the darkness.

This time it reflected for an instant in a pair of widely spaced green eyes. A tawny shadow, just a glimpse, merged with the trees.

Sam seized the cool end of one blazing treetop. He ran to the place, maybe thirty feet from the fire, where he had seen the shadow, screaming and whirling the burning club around over his head. A comet's tail of sparks followed the end of the club.

Mac ran around Sam, barking a hoarse challenge. Dad must have sent him to help. Nose to the ground, the dog tracked the scent up the slope. Sam whistled Mac to his side and, still holding the torch over his head, ran back to the camp.

His father stood poised, silhouetted against the fire. As Sam neared him, his shouts rose, muffled by the falls' noise but audible. He whistled a piercing blast, and another, his knife ready in his hand.

Dad might mistake Sam for the pouncing cat. A few feet away, Sam whistled back and then embraced his father. "Sit down, Dad. We're all okay."

Sam replaced the pine torch in the fire and added another treetop. He returned to the bed and lay down beside his father and Mac, gasping for air, his heart crashing against his ribs. All three of them panted. All three trembled.

Dad, trembling again, and not from tired muscles this time.

Dad, afraid.

"What happened? I still can't see."

Sam couldn't answer. He had never seen his father afraid before he had jumped the crevice earlier that day. He had always been Superman, more powerful than a locomotive, faster than a speeding bullet, fearless and impervious to everything but Kryptonite. But Dad trembled now.

"He's gone," Sam gasped. "A cat. A big one."

"You *saw* him?"

"He saw us first. He was out there watching us."

"You're sure? It wasn't just a bobcat? Not a nightmare?"

"You don't believe me? Criminy! I saw his green eyes."

If the cougar had been a dream cat, then Mac had dreamed him, too. Sam had seen the cougar with his own eyes—he knew he had. He had saved all of them, and now Dad doubted him.

Sam would prove that the cat was real. "Just a minute," he said. "I won't go far."

"No! Stay in camp."

Sam picked up the flashlight in one hand and the fiery torch in the other and walked with shaky steps toward the steep wooded slope he and his father had descended that afternoon. It was the place where his father had rested with no protection while Sam scouted, where not so long ago he had gathered firewood and pine boughs, leaving his father with only a knife. Now Sam wasn't just trembling; his whole body shook. The beam of the light jigged in his hand.

Beyond the firelight he found the first track in the rime that covered the rocks between the river and the slope. The surface was a little slippery. Sam's own footprints had smeared other tracks nearby. Mac nudged his legs, but Sam ignored him, searching for the mountain lion's trail. And there it was, coming from the spring. The cat had walked on only three feet. The frost told the story.

Sam followed the trail toward the camp to a smooth spot where the cat had sat on its haunches, watching them long enough to melt the frost. There were the marks left by its hindquarters and the swish of its long tail. There were the prints of both front paws. One track was bloody.

Sam rushed back to his father, who stood as close as possible to the fire.

"What?" Sam's father's voice and the knife in his hand were shaking.

"He's walking on three feet," said Sam. "Other one's bloody. Maybe cut."

"He's hungry, then," his father said. "Game is too fast for a three-legged cat. We're slower than other game."

Other game. They were prey. Sam had known, but now the knowledge sank in. He shook off the words and looked at his father's watch in the firelight. "Only *eleven?*"

Daylight would not dawn for six hours, and the cat was still out there.

Watching.

Chapter 7

AS THEY STOOD TOGETHER, SAM drew in a ragged breath, unable to tell Dad any more. Downstream the waterfall roared. His father took him in his trembling arms. Saying nothing, he just held him. Suddenly, Sam's legs could no longer hold him up. He collapsed onto his sore knees.

His father knelt with him. "Tell me everything."

"I woke up." What Sam had seen unrolled in his mind, vivid, like a slow-motion scene in a movie. "Mac barked. The cat's eyes were green. I chased him away with a torch from the fire."

"Brave boy. Smart, too." Sam's father embraced him again. "Where's Mac?"

"Policing the camp." Sam held his father as if their lives depended upon their becoming a single body.

"Where's the hatchet?"

"Dropped it. I'll find it in the morning."

"What a dumb—"

Here came the accusations. Sam was a jackass and a fool. But no—Dad stopped the insults before they began.

"Never mind," he said, rising to his feet. "Things happen. Now we need to plan together."

"I'll watch," said Sam. "This time I won't fall asleep."

"I've already slept several hours," his father said. "I'll keep Mac by me. If the cat comes back, Mac will signal me. I'll wake you."

Sam lay back on the lumpy bed. He had

been brave, Dad had said. He was smart. Dad trusted Sam and would wake him up if the cat came back. The words were sweet, but still Sam wasn't certain of himself. What if the mountain lion surprised them tomorrow, when they would not have the protection of the fire?

"I'm too jumpy to sleep," he said.

"Never mind," said his father. "Just lie there awhile."

Sam tossed on the lumpy bed—he would never sleep now. The next thing he knew, though, he was reliving his pursuit of the cougar in a nightmare. This time the cat did not run away but turned and fought. Sam's own shout woke him up.

"Be cool, boyo," said his father, shaking him. "We're all right."

Mac sat with Dad, wrapped in the flimsy blanket.

Sam stood up beside them. "Your turn, Mac," he said. "Lie down. Go to sleep."

"Yes. Sleep, our good old Mac. Long day tomorrow."

Sam's father petted Mac until he fell asleep. "What's the time?" He held out his wrist.

Sam looked at the watch. "Four."

"Daybreak in half an hour or so. We'll leave as soon as it's light enough for us to see in the shadows." A moment's silence. "Until *you* can see."

Sam found his father's backpack and divided the food into fifths. His stomach growled with hunger. He kept one fifth for himself, gave one to his father, and put aside half of another for Mac. The rest he stowed in his own pack, amazed by how little food had ever mattered until now.

"What's left?"

"Fifty percent. Enough for lunch."

"You're a pretty good planner."

Three compliments in one night—Sam didn't know if he could stand so much praise.

"Take me to the river's edge," said Dad. "I'll fill the water pack."

Sam picked up a torch from the fire, Dad placed his hand on Sam's shoulder, and they made their way to the riverside, with Mac close behind.

"Brr," Sam said, stepping carefully so he wouldn't slip on a frosty rock. "The cat scared me so much last night, I didn't pay attention to the cold. Windbreakers and light fleece aren't good enough."

"You were scared?"

Light from the torch shone in the river and illuminated the planes of Dad's face.

"Well, not really scared—" Sam began to say.

"I was scared, too. You'd be crazy not to be scared," said his father. "And this cold—yeah, the rocks are so cold, the mist from the water-fall sticks. Temperature must have dropped quite a bit below freezing. That's the end of our vegetable garden, and it's only August."

"How can you think about tomatoes now?"

"After the way I've nursed them along all summer with cold frames and heaters and covers? I *like* tomatoes." Sam's father snorted. "Besides, I need a break from stark raving terror."

When they had refilled the water packs, they returned to the fire. Dad rearranged both space blankets around them all. "Keep your fire at the ready, Sam. I have my knife." He shook the hunting knife in his hand. "And here's my shillelagh." The blackthorn stick lay near.

They sat together, sharing their three bodies' warmth until the eastern sky lightened. Still they waited, until the dawn was bright enough for Sam to see, even under the trees on the slope.

Sam had fed the fire again and again. Three fourths of the wood was gone—good thing he had dragged in more than he thought they needed. Now, where was that hatchet?

He found it under a log that must have rolled onto it when he had moved another piece of wood. He shoved the hatchet handle into his jeans again. He had already folded the ground cloth and the space blankets and stowed them. Then he transferred all the gear from Dad's backpack into his own, leaving out only the silvery blankets. Sam would carry the weight.

Before they left camp, he used a heavy branch to scatter the embers among the broken rocks. He dragged the burning saplings to the river, plunged them underwater, and left them on the bank to avoid any possibility of a forest fire.

Despite the work, both he and his father were shivering. Their breath rose in a cloud around their heads. Sam cut X-shaped holes in the space blankets, making ponchos to keep them warm while they hiked.

"Here, Dad. Put your head through this hole. Now, let me see your eyes."

Sam's father turned. "Hurt like hell."

"Don't swear," said Sam, but his stomach turned over with guilt. His father was merely stating a fact. Both of his eyes were red and swollen almost shut. Yet he didn't complain. Something yellow had collected in the inner corners and dried. Dad rubbed it away. Even if he could have stood the glare, he couldn't open his eyes wide enough to see much.

Sam wanted to say how sorry he was, longed for more kind words, but he guarded himself. In a moment, his father reminded him why.

"Here's the strategy." Sam's father tied his bandanna around his eyes again. He was taking charge once more.

"Let's wait until we're far enough from the falls to talk without yelling," Sam said in his father's ear.

"Are you afraid the cat will hear our plans?" He snickered at the joke. Blind or not, he was the same old Dad. "Where's the hatchet?"

"At my waist. Do you suppose you could let me have the sheath?"

Sam's father unbuckled his belt and handed over the leather holster for the hatchet. "It isn't easy to give over control," he said with a sigh.

"I never would've guessed," said Sam. He threaded the sheath onto his own belt, checked for his knife in his pocket, and shouldered his backpack. He had already planned the route they would take. Beyond the waterfall, the river raced in a cut worn between vertical walls that would force them to backtrack in many places. "We'll climb the slope upstream this time. The grade is easier there."

Talking into each other's ears, they had to

touch. Sam gave his father a quick, awkward hug.

His father's return hug was awkward, too. He sheathed his hunting knife, but he didn't snap the leather catch. He shouldered his pack and placed one hand on Sam's shoulder. "You've taken the weight in your own pack."

"It isn't much."

Sam led his father along the edge of the woods while Mac ran ahead to scout, staying always within sight. Their feet and the stick and the dog left a black trail behind them in the frost. The cougar's tracks were still visible ahead, though not as clear as they had been in the night, when they were fresh. The cat had followed the edge of the woods, too.

Soon Sam and his father came to the sandy bed of the spring. They were far enough now from the falls to hear the other's normal voice, and here the rocks were bare of frost.

"No ice here, away from the falls," said

Sam. "At least we won't slip. Now we're turning right, Dad. Maybe we'll go easier along this little creek."

The grade was much more gentle here, as Sam had thought. He picked his way between boulders and trees. When the slope flattened out at the top, Sam veered right again, looking for a clearing where he could see all the way around them. The cat would look for cover. It might even attack them in daylight, like the starving female that had knocked a cyclist off her bike a few years ago and dragged her into the woods. Sam had read about the incident on the Internet. Several other riders had saved the woman, but now she was blind in one eye, and the scars on her face had required plastic surgery several times. Sam watched on all sides and kept an eye on Mac's behavior, too.

"The strategy," said Sam's father.

"When I find a safe place to rest," said Sam.

"Okay."

They made their way between big firs. Sam's father proceeded now on his own with his stick, often belly-crawling down the side of a boulder, or sitting, to scoot safely down a slope. His silvery poncho was ripped, and blood had soaked the edges of a hole worn in one knee of his jeans.

"Here's a clearing," said Sam when they came to a broad expanse of limestone with nothing growing but scabby lichen and a few grasses in cracks. "We'll sit in the middle, where Mac and I can watch."

They sat down together and folded their legs. Mac joined them.

"He doesn't want to be left out of the strategy," said Sam's father, scratching the collie's black ears. He rummaged in the packs and handed Sam the compass. "Right, then. Just follow the mountain down. That's all we need to do. Use the compass to make sure we hit the road."

"I don't want to, either," said Sam.

"What do you mean, you don't want to? You know how to use a compass."

"No. I don't want to be left out of the strategy."

His father went on as if he were deaf. "Trouble is, that cat won't have forgotten us. Especially since he's injured. Watch out for overhangs where he could ambush us. Keep your eyes peeled."

"Yeah, Dad." Nobody in the history of the world had ever known as much as Dad. "I'm already avoiding overhangs. Making plans, too," Sam said.

"You have a plan? What do you want to do?"

What did Sam want to do? How long he had waited for that question from Dad. Months. Years. "What I want to do . . ." Sam breathed. What he wanted to do was choose for himself whether to play his music or hike with Dad. For now, though, he was taking charge again. "What we're going to do is follow the slope down. I'll use the sun and the slope as my compass. If we head north as well as east, we'll hit that old logging road. Remember? We'll have to hike pretty far out of our way, and we'll have to leave the river, but the road will take us down."

"Sam, you're nobody's fool."

"It's about time you noticed," Sam said. "On the diagonal, the grade will be easier. The hike will be farther, but it'll be hours faster in the end."

The sun and the effort had warmed them now, though their breath was still visible. They removed their makeshift ponchos; Sam folded them and put them at the top of his pack, just in case.

"I don't remember any streams between here and that logging road," said Dad.

"Maybe we'll hit a spring. And we have enough water to last at least through the day."

"I guess you've thought of everything, Sam. Lead on, my man. Lead on."

A burden lifted. Dad had acknowledged his dependence on Sam. At least he wouldn't have to fight his father.

Chapter 8

BY NOON THE ROCKS HE HAD slid down had worn through the hip pockets of Sam's father's jeans. His white underwear, ragged now, showed through the holes. His backside was bleeding. Tears in the denim exposed both bloody knees, scraped when he slid down on his stomach, and one sleeve of his windbreaker was torn from wrist to elbow. His muscles quivered.

"Here's a good place to rest," said Sam, taking his father's hand.

"I can keep going."

"Dad, this isn't a contest. Your hands look

like hamburger." Sam took his father's left wrist to look at his watch. What if they were lost? "Nearly noon. Do you think we overshot that logging road?"

"No—remember, everything we do takes twice as long as usual."

"Three times, at least." Sam propelled his father to a footstool-size boulder in the sun. Although the shadows still were cool, they were sweating now. They shed their jackets and fleeces, and Sam stowed them in his pack with everything else.

"Sit," he said.

"Yes, master." Sam's father sat and put his blackthorn down. "Where's our Mac?" He whistled a shrill call, but Mac did not respond.

The dog had strayed while Sam wasn't looking. He felt a pang of nervousness, but it quickly faded. Mac had been there just a moment before, and he wouldn't go far.

Sam inspected one of his father's hands. Fresh bright blood trickled over dark old blood that had dried in his palm. Rocks had gouged long scratches and rubbed blisters that had broken and wept on the heel of his hand and the pads of his fingers. Yet his father had never peeped a complaint.

"Dad! Why didn't you tell me how bad your hands were? I would have wrapped them up a long time ago."

"They're just scratched. They'll heal."

Sam cursed.

"Don't swear," said Dad.

"I'll swear if I damn well want to!" said Sam. "This is dumb. You always have to be tougher than anybody else, and then you make me match you. 'Keep up with the rest of us, Sam.' You've been telling me that since I was five years old. 'You're crying about *that* little thing?' That's what you said when the jellyfish stung me in Florida." His words a flood, Sam was yelling now. The yelling felt good.

"We have to get down off the mountain," Dad said. "Complaining isn't going to help."

"Yeah, but you expect everybody else to be like you," Sam answered. "Me. Mom. Even your patients, after you've sawed through their bones and messed with their insides."

"Yes. Well. They recover fast then, don't they?"

Sam's bluster had worn itself out. "You're some piece of work, Dad. Your hands must hurt so much." He gently removed three tiny stones that were embedded in a scratch and wrapped a bandanna around each of his father's hands.

"I hear water."

Sam listened. "Yeah. Down that slope. Give me your pack and I'll go refill it just in case."

"Where's our Mac?" Dad whistled again using his thumb and finger.

Where *was* Mac, anyway? Sam whistled, too, listened, and watched, but Mac had disappeared again.

"Keep a sharp eye," his father said.

"You, too." Sam handed his father the hatchet. Then he put the straps of both packs over one shoulder and opened his biggest jackknife blade. With the pump in his other hand, he followed the sound of the water. At the foot of the steep grade, a trickling stream flowed over the lip of a rocky shelf and fell five feet to a pool with a sandy bottom. Above the pool, the ground was boggy where the water flowed from a spring. Sam looked around for Mac and whistled again. Where *was* that dog?

As Sam filled the water bladders, Mac emerged from the trees above, onto the boggy shelf. Limping, he picked his way down the slope to Sam.

"What happened to you, boy?" Sam said. As he sloshed water on Mac's bleeding snout, what had happened became obvious. A claw had scored the dog's muzzle, and something was wrong with one hind leg.

"Dad!" Sam shouted. "Watch out!" He shouldered the packs again. "Come," he said to Mac.

Sam scrambled back up the slope, glancing back at every other step. Mac lagged, so Sam put his knife in his pocket and went back a few steps. He hefted Mac onto one hip. The dog whined, but he didn't struggle to get down, as he ordinarily would have. Holding Mac with both arms now, Sam struggled back up the hill, shouting to scare the cougar away.

By the time Sam reached the hilltop, his lungs were bursting. His father stood, his hatchet in one hand, making his silhouette as big as he could and swinging his blackthorn.

"We're here, Dad," Sam called. "Mac's had a run-in with the cat. Clawed muzzle. Hurt hind leg." He set the dog down at his father's feet.

"Bloody Nora."

"Don't swear. Or at least swear in American."

"Bloody Nora isn't swearing in Glasgow. Cat doesn't give up, does he? Must be starved."

Sam handed his father the water pack, but he set it down beside him. He made that little kissing noise he always used to coax Mac to his side and examined the dog's leg with sure hands. Mac whined, but he let Sam's father explore the bones.

Sam looked around the clearing at all the places where a cougar could hide—the high rock faces, the brush. Now would be a good time for the x-ray vision to kick in. Bloody Nora was right. He cursed that he had only ordinary boy vision, just ordinary boy instincts and judgment and strength. He kicked at a rock and hurt his toe. Despair, his father would say, would do no good.

"Don't think it's broken," said his father. "Just a light splint will do." He removed the bandanna that bound his left hand. After cutting the hem with his knife, he tore the bandanna, working around the edges in a spiral, slightly cutting the inside corners, until he had a continuous strip of cloth. As sure of himself as if he could see, he bound Mac's leg, split the end of the cloth, and tied it. Sam wished his own knowledge were as certain and his hands as deft.

"There. That'll help."

"His nose," said Sam.

Sam watched as his father felt Mac's muzzle and head. Here was a side of Dad that Sam hadn't seen in years, not since he was a little boy and Dad bound up his scraped knees and turned ankles. Dad had gentle hands and experience that knew what his hands were feeling for. He had kindness, too, that tried to do no hurt. This gentleness had been there all along.

"Do you see any spurting blood?" Sam's father asked.

"No. He's still bleeding some, but he licks the blood away. No spurts."

"I can feel how swollen his face is," Dad said. "You're probably right—the cat. Whatever he is, he packs some clout, but Mac'll be okay if we can get him home today."

Mac lay down beside Sam's father. Dad watered Mac before he himself would drink.

"I left the pump by the spring," Sam said.

"Here." Sam's father handed the hatchet to him. "Keep it in your hand."

"What if the cat's down there?"

"Keep your wits about you, and yell. I'll

shout, too. And don't run—cats chase runners. Instinct."

Sam couldn't do it—he just couldn't go back down to that pool, where the lion might be waiting. He couldn't. Nevertheless, they had to have water; they needed the pump. He held the hatchet handle near the head. One foot forward, then the other. He couldn't go alone. Last night had been just a reflex. He was a sissy, after all. At every step he looked all around. The cat would need water, too. He could be drinking now in the pool at the bottom of the slope. Still, Sam gathered courage with every step. Nearing the pool, he stopped to watch for a moment. No cat. Not even a frog or a water strider. There was the pump, where he had dropped it. He picked it up, eyes and ears and every muscle tensed and every hair at attention, and hurried back up the slope to his father.

"Whew!" Sam smiled despite himself. He was no sissy. What had he been thinking? "We'll eat before we go," he said.

His father had cut the long sleeves from his shirt and wrapped his hands with them. Sam gave Mac and his father their portions of food and took his own. Although Mac whimpered when he chewed, he ate.

Now the food was gone.

Sam's father stood. "What a bunch," he said. "Two cripples and a kid. Let's move."

At least he hadn't said "two cripples and a baby." He hadn't said "sissy." Sam shouldered his pack, took his father's hand, and began again to find the way home.

Chapter 9

BUSHWHACKING HAD NEVER been so scary. Never so exhausting.

"Do you think cougars have tracked us before? On other hikes, I mean," Sam asked.

"Probably. They're sneaky critters. We just happen to know this one is there, and he knows we're hurt. They rarely bother people, though."

A shiver spread through Sam as he remembered all the overhanging shelves he had walked beneath, all the boulders he had skirted where a mountain lion might have waited to pounce. "Look sharp," his father had said, as if

Sam were anything like relaxed. He felt as if his eyes rotated on stalks, and new ones had grown in the back of his head. Now Mac, as well as his father, was dependent on him. Where was that dog, again? He had been here just a moment ago.

"Where's Mac?" Sam said. "Mac!"

Sam and his father both whistled shrill calls.

"Should have made a leash for him—there! There he is," Sam said as Mac's black tail disappeared around a boulder.

"Not your fault," said Sam's father.

"I'll go after him."

"No!"

"Have to—or he's cat food." Sam was already moving.

"Eyes sharp! Eyes sharp!"

Sam ran across the level clearing, backtracking, imagining Mac in the cat's jaws.

"Eyes sharp!" Dad called.

And there came Mac's bark and the high-pitched scream Sam had feared, scarier than any sound he had ever heard, and, an instant later, a yelp—Mac's tenor yelp. Shouting, Sam ran toward the snarling and the scuffling sounds of a fight, the hatchet in his hand. And there, around a rock face Sam and Dad had just passed was the cougar, with Mac's haunch in its mouth. It was dragging him down the rocky hillside toward a stand of firs.

Mac looked like a toy in the cougar's teeth, but he had not given up. He struggled in the animal's clutch, squirming and twisting his body around to bite the big cat's face, its jaw, its throat. At last he clamped the cougar's nose in his teeth and shook his head until the cat dropped him and reared, snarling, its lips drawn back to expose long teeth. Mac struggled to his feet.

Sam sprinted down the slope toward the cat,

shouting, the hatchet raised above his head. His first swing missed by a mile, carrying him off balance. The cougar charged and knocked Sam down with a swipe of a paw, but Mac leapt onto the cat's back, tore its ear, and rolled away. Sam regained his footing and swung the hatchet again.

Again. And again. Far away, something was barking. No, not far away. Right here at Sam's feet, the little dog barked and then bit the cougar's leg and held on. Then, as if Sam had practiced forever to make this movement, the hatchet blade connected with the cougar's head. Sam heard the loud crack of shattered bone. The cougar fell onto Mac and knocked him down. In a rush of rage, Sam struck the cougar one more fierce blow. Then he fell in a heap of cougar, dog, and boy, all piled together.

Sam scrambled away. Mac struggled from under the heavy cat and barked a hoarse yip, nudging at Sam, still trying to herd him to safety. Gasping for breath, his heart wild, Sam stumbled to his feet. What if the cat was still alive? What if he regained consciousness and attacked again? Where was the hatchet? Sam had lost the damn thing again. There— Staggering, he retrieved his weapon, but the cat did not move. Sam poked the tail with the toe of his boot. He picked up a heavy foot and let it fall. His hands were still shaking.

Up the hill, Dad was shouting. Mac was bloody. Sam fell panting at his side and felt the dog's body for wounds. Blood oozed from a crescent of puncture wounds the cougar's teeth had made, clear through Mac's right haunch, but the rest of the blood was the cat's. Despite his injuries, Mac stood up. He was shaking, too.

Dad yelled from the top of the slope. "Sam! Sam! Where are you?"

"Here, Dad," Sam called back. "We're okay." Was he really okay? He felt himself for wounds. His shirt sleeve had been torn off, and claws had gouged his upper arm, but the scratches weren't deep. "We're okay!"

Sam replaced the bloody hatchet in its sheath on his belt. Carrying Mac, he stumbled back up the rise and met his father at the rock wall. The bandanna was up on his forehead, and he squinted through slitted eyelids, still shouting. He carried his blackthorn in one hand and his knife in the other, coming to the aid of Sam and Mac despite his blindness.

"I'm here, Dad." Sam put Mac down. For the second time in one day—or was it the third?—Sam willingly embraced his father.

"No. Back against the wall. The cat may charge again."

"It's over," Sam said.

"What? What's over?"

"Cat's dead."

"You're sure?"

"His head's caved in," said Sam.

His father clutched him and made a most terrible moan, his shoulders shaking. He was sobbing.

"I'm sorry, Dad, so sorry I hurt you." Sam was crying, too.

His father patted Sam's shoulders. "It was an accident. I shouldn't have followed so close. Sorry I yelled at you."

They stepped away from each other and wiped their eyes. With the sorrys out of the way, Sam relaxed.

"Now, tell your blinky old Dad what happened. Are you hurt?" Dad ran his fingers over Sam's face.

Sam felt his sticky arm where the cat had clawed him. His jeans were torn, and a big purple bruise was forming on his thigh, but

Dad didn't need anything more to worry about. "I'm fine," Sam said.

"Mac couldn't have killed him. What happened?"

"I did. Killed him, I mean. The hatchet."

"Good grief, Sam."

Mac whined. Sam's father knelt and coaxed the dog near. He felt every inch of Mac's body. "We're his herd. He was protecting us. He's a hero, too, our Mac." He continued his examination. "Blood here, but no fractures, I reckon."

They took off their packs and set them down by Mac, who lay more still than Sam had ever seen him. Sam led his father to the cougar. Flies already swarmed around the animal's head and crawled over its closed eyes. A black shadow crossed in front of Sam and continued in an arc. A pair of bald eagles circled overhead against the perfect blue sky. The next animals in the food chain had found their afternoon meal. Without a doubt the coyotes were already watching.

"Where's his head?" his father asked.

Sam placed the blackthorn by the cougar's bloody head, and his father prodded it. It rolled to a grotesque angle from its body.

"Tell me the rest," said Dad.

Sam still had not caught his breath. "Cat caught Mac. Dragged him toward those trees down there. I went after him."

Now Sam's father knelt and turned his exploring hands to the cougar.

Sam crouched and stroked the animal's white muzzle and throat. He turned the great crushed head so he couldn't see the hatchet wounds. He traced the black edges of the ears and the dark stripes on the pearly muzzle with his forefinger. He straightened the legs and curled the long tail around the body, as if the tail could protect it. "I had to do it," he said, wiping his eyes again with the heels of his hands. "He would have killed Mac."

"Of course you had to. He would have killed us, too. Doesn't mean you shouldn't be sad."

"He's so beautiful, Dad."

Sam's father ran his fingertips over the cougar's torso. "She. Female. So she is. Magnificent creature—must be seven or eight feet long, counting her tail." He felt for her paws. "Which one was bloody—her tracks by the river?"

"Right front, I think."

Sam's father picked up her paw, weighed it in his bandaged hand, and examined it by touch. It was bigger than his palm. "Look at that," he said. "Two toes torn off, and some other bones are broken. They kept the wound open. And see how thin she is. Ticks have

sucked her dry, and she hasn't had a decent
meal since she was hurt."

The cougar had been starving, then. Her
life had depended on her killing Mac, and she
had made a brave attempt.

"Pity to waste her beautiful pelt," Sam's
father said. "Do you want it?"

"No!" said Sam. "I want to bury her. Give
her a proper funeral."

"What time is it, Sam?"

Sam looked at Dad's watch. "Nearly two
thirty."

"What do you think?" his father asked.

Sam looked up at the eagles, drawing their
lazy circles, waiting. "I want to bury her, but
wanting doesn't count for much. We have to
go."

"We can come back up here with a shovel
in a couple days, when my eyes have healed."

"No," said Sam. "We should just let the

mountain have her. You know she'll be gone by then, anyway. Some other hungry animals will find her."

Sam's father rubbed his whiskers with his raggedy hand. "You may be sure of it. Hurt and hunger everywhere." His voice broke. Clumsy with feeling, he pulled Sam to him again. After a moment, he cleared his throat and let Sam go. "Better get crackin'."

"Just a minute." Dad's hug had made Sam wince. He felt almost too weak to stand, but he stumbled down among the firs. He cut several green boughs with the hatchet. The cougar's dry blood still dyed the steel maroon. When the hatchet was securely snapped in its sheath again, Sam dragged the boughs back up the hill and spread them out over the cougar's body.

His father felt for the boughs and tried to help.

Sam wiped the sticky sap on his jeans; it was nothing. They climbed back up the hill to the rock wall, where Sam knelt beside Mac. "Come on, boyo. We're going home."

"Wait a minute," said Dad. "Let me have your pack."

"No. Mac needs a ride." Sam transferred the gear to Dad's pack and gently eased Mac into his own, letting the dog's head poke out through an opening in the zipper.

Dad helped Sam heft the pack onto his shoulders. "That's a load of dog. Thirty pounds, anyway. Good thing he's a runt. I'll spell you when you need a break."

"I can do it," said Sam. He did not feel as sure as he sounded.

Chapter 10

AFTER SEVERAL MORE HOURS OF hard trudging, they came to the logging road, just as Sam had planned. The dirt road switched back and forth across the face of the mountain, leading them down toward the paved road and the valley town. They were still miles from the place where they had left the car, but neither of them could drive, anyway. If they reached the pavement soon, some passerby would see them. Somebody would offer them a ride, for sure. They wouldn't have to sleep out-doors again. Would they?

Sam and his father had said hardly anything

since the cougar attack, too tired and out of breath to find the air for conversation. Perhaps Dad needed time to absorb all that had happened, just as Sam did.

When neither of them could walk another step without a break, they stopped. They backed up to a boulder and rested their packs on it, too tired to take them off, and then to sit, and then to get up and shoulder the packs again. Every movement hurt.

Mac didn't make a sound; maybe he was asleep.

"I'm going to keep climbing up this mountain, you know," Dad said when he had caught his breath.

"Yup," said Sam. "Next time bring a cell phone."

"You're a good climbing partner."

"I know," said Sam. "But I'm going to keep playing guitar, too."

"Yup," said Dad. "I'll be listening."

Sam didn't want to hope too much that things had changed for good. He turned his head to check on Mac, and the dog gave him a slurpy kiss. Then they all were so still that a red squirrel ran down an aspen branch right by Sam's face. The tiny squirrel stared at Sam. Sam stared back. Then the creature suddenly realized what Sam was. It squeaked, "*Eep*," jumped straight up in the air, scampered back up the branch, and disappeared.

Sam burst out laughing.

"What was that?" Dad asked.

"A red squirrel," Sam replied

A moment later the squirrel appeared again in the aspen above them, scolding with a voice far too big for its body.

"I guess he means it's time to hit the road," said Dad.

The squirrel chittered again.

"We're *leaving*," said Sam. "Good-*bye*."

———

Before dark had fallen on the mountain, they reached the pavement. The muscles in Sam's legs quivered, his shoulders screamed, and his feet were concrete blocks, but he walked. Lift. Lurch. Lift again. Neither of them would ever make it all the way to town. They might not even make it around that curve up ahead.

Mac whined. Then an engine chugged, laboring as it climbed. A green pickup flashed between the trees on a switchback below. Maybe the driver was a ranger. A laugh started in Sam's belly and burbled up through his chest. Dad laughed, too. In a moment, though, their laughter sounded a lot like sobs. They leaned together, each holding the other up until the truck approached.

Sam stumbled into the road with his thumb out. The driver slowed to give them an appraising look as he passed. Sam held his breath. Then the truck made a quick U-turn and pulled up right beside them. The door opened, and the man climbed out and hurried around the front of the truck, his arms out-stretched to help.

"Come on, Dad." Sam took his father's elbow, and they hobbled arm in arm toward the stranger who would take them home.

ABOUT THE AUTHOR

Jane Resh Thomas has written many books for Clarion and is the recipient of the 2001 Kerlan Award for "singular attainment in the creation of children's literature." When she isn't writing about nature, she is usually enjoying it, whether in her garden or on more rugged turf. Ms. Thomas teaches writing at Vermont College and in Minneapolis, Minnesota, where she lives.